A GIRL, a BOY, and a MONSTER CAT

A GIRL, a BOY, and a MONSTER CAT

GAIL GAUTHIER

illustrated by JOE CEPEDA

G. P. PUTNAM'S SONS

G. P. PUTNAM'S SONS
A division of Penguin Young Readers Group. Published by The Penguin Group.
Penguin Group (USA) Inc., 375 Hudson Street, New York, NY 10014, U.S.A.

Penguin Group (Canada), 90 Eglinton Avenue East, Suite 700, Toronto, Ontario, Canada
M4P 2Y3 (a division of Pearson Penguin Canada Inc.). Penguin Books Ltd, 80 Strand, London
WC2R 0RL, England. Penguin Ireland, 25 St. Stephen's Green, Dublin 2, Ireland (a division of
Penguin Books Ltd.). Penguin Group (Australia), 250 Camberwell Road, Camberwell, Victoria
3124, Australia (a division of Pearson Australia Group Pty Ltd). Penguin Books India Pvt Ltd,
11 Community Centre, Panchsheel Park, New Delhi - 110 017, India. Penguin Group (NZ),
Cnr Airborne and Rosedale Roads, Albany, Auckland 1310, New Zealand (a division of Pearson
New Zealand Ltd). Penguin Books (South Africa) (Pty) Ltd, 24 Sturdee Avenue, Rosebank,
Johannesburg 2196, South Africa. Penguin Books Ltd, Registered Offices: 80 Strand, London
WC2R 0RL, England.

Published simultaneously in Canada. Printed
in the United States of America. Design by Gina DiMassi. Text set in Mendoza Roman.
Library of Congress Cataloging-in-Publication Data Gauthier, Gail, 1953– A girl, a boy, and
a monster cat / Gail Gauthier ; illustrated by Joe Cepeda. p. cm. Summary: Three afternoons
a week, Brandon reluctantly stays with his imaginative classmate, Hannah, and her oversized
cat, Buttercup, playing games, but their adventures really begin when a new neighbor moves
in with a ferocious Chihuahua named Bucky. [1. Play—Fiction. 2. Imagination—Fiction.
3. Cats—Fiction. 4. Chihuahua (Dog breed)—Fiction. 5. Dogs—Fiction.] I. Cepeda, Joe, ill.
II. Title. PZ7.G23435Gir 2007 [Fic]—dc22 2006020530
ISBN 978-0-399-24689-0
1 3 5 7 9 10 8 6 4 2
First Impression

For my niece, Rebecca,
and her uncle Russell

Contents

THE
HANNAH CLUB

Chapter 1

Hannah Dufrane stood up. She was moving slowly, as if it were hard work. That's because she always makes a great big deal about everything. You'd think she had just climbed up the side of a building or something. She had her long, dark hair stuck up under her dad's wool hat that he wears in the winter. She had a flashlight in her hand. She was gasping for breath.

All that just to look over the top of the sofa in her family room. Really. That was all she was doing.

When she was finally on her feet, she turned to where I was hiding behind a chair. That was the sign for me to stand up, too.

I thought it was, anyway. By the time she got around to me, I wasn't sure I still remembered the sign. It didn't matter, though. I don't have to worry about forgetting things when I'm with Hannah. She remembers everything, and she likes telling me what to do.

We were spying on a cat. He was creeping toward the stand where Hannah's mom keeps all her fanciest plants. You couldn't miss him. He was on the floor right in front of us. Spying on him was an easy job.

But Hannah doesn't like easy jobs. She likes what *she* calls games. Her games are like really bad TV shows. Only you can't turn the channel to something better because you're part of the show.

She makes me play them with her on Monday, Wednesday, and Friday afternoons. That's when I have to go to her house even though I've already spent the entire day with her at school.

"Brandon, it's a perfect plan," Mom said to me

when she arranged for Mrs. D. to take care of me three afternoons a week. "Hannah will have someone to play with, and you'll have a place to go while I'm at work."

The perfect plan would have been for me to go to Sam Clark's house. His family has a big-screen TV that they keep on *all* the time. Plus, Sam is a boy, and I am a boy. Anyone can see that I should be at Sam's house three times a week. But Mom wouldn't even ask Sam's mother if I could stay there. Even though I told her about the big-screen TV.

Instead, I'm stuck with Hannah.

Hannah knelt down behind her sofa again, which was kind of confusing. I wasn't sure what I was supposed to do. So I got down on my hands and knees and hurried over to join her.

"What do we do now?" I asked.

"Be quiet," Hannah ordered. "The enemy will hear you."

"The enemy's just a cat," I said.

"He's not *just* a cat," she told me. "He's a *monster* cat that will eat all the plants in the world if we let him."

As if that would ever happen. One cat, even a monster cat, would never be able to eat all the plants in the world.

"Does the monster cat eat lettuce and cucumbers?" I asked. Because maybe a monster cat could eat all of just two kinds of plants. "I hate lettuce and cucumbers. He can eat all the lettuce and cucumbers he wants."

Hannah got this look on her face as if I'd burped in church or something. On purpose. After she was finished looking disgusted, she said, "If no one stops him, he will bring *more* monster cats. They will eat *all* the plants in the world. There will be *no* grass and *no* leaves on the trees. *No* flowers."

"If those monster cats promise to eat all the lettuce and cucumbers, they can *have* the leaves and the flowers," I replied.

"I am the boss here, Brandon, and I say they can't."

Hannah always gets to be the boss. She used to have a club at school with some girls who played her games with her during recess. She was always the boss there, too. But one of the girls joined another club where everybody made hair clips with beads and glue. Then the other two girls made their own club for drawing pictures of fairies.

Hannah was a member of that club for two days, but she got bored doing the same thing all the time. Now during recess she reads books and thinks of games for us to play at her house. It's as if my mother signed me up for some kind of Hannah Club. And I'm the only member.

She picked up a paper from the floor.

"Is that the map you drew or the one I drew?" I asked.

"The one I drew."

"Where's mine?"

"I left it in the kitchen," Hannah said.

"Why?"

"Because we only need one, and mine is better," she replied.

"If we only needed one, why did you make me draw one, too?" I asked. "I could have drawn a snowman."

"We're playing *spy*, Brandon. Remember? You don't draw snowmen when you're playing *spy*."

"I could have drawn a snowspy," I suggested.

"But we're spying in the house today," Hannah insisted. "We couldn't use a snowspy in the house. Save that for sometime when we're spying outdoors. You can draw a snowspy, and then we'll go outside and make it."

"We'd have to be spying outdoors in the winter, I guess," I said.

"Yes, we would. People will know right off that something is wrong if you have a snowspy at any other time of year."

I had to admit that building a snowspy in April didn't seem like the kind of thing a good spy should do.

Hannah used a red crayon to mark an X on the map.

"What's the X for?" I asked.

"The X is for the spot where we found the monster cat. See? I put the X in front of the plant stand," she explained.

I pointed to another place on the map and said, "I think he was over a little bit more this way. You need to move the X."

"No, I don't. He was right where I said he was. Look, I'll show you."

Hannah stood up, so I figured I could, too.

"See? Oops. Where did he go?" she asked. "Oh, no! He's on the plant stand eating one of Mom's plants!"

"I'll save it!" I said.

I love saving things.

I climbed over the back of the sofa, bounced off the seat, and landed in the middle of the room. While I was doing it, I went, "Aaaaaaaa!" because guys on TV shout when they're jumping off things. They sound really cool.

"No, Brandon!" Hannah called as she ran around the sofa. "You can't yell when you're spying! You'll scare the enemy away."

The enemy didn't look scared to me. He just sat on the plant stand with the end of a long skinny leaf hanging out of the side of his mouth while he chewed and chewed and chewed on it. He was getting cat spit all over the thing.

"That is *so* gross," I said.

"You wrecked the game," Hannah complained. "You asked too many questions, so we didn't see the enemy attack. Then you made too much noise. You let the enemy know we were here."

"The enemy doesn't care," I pointed out. "See? He looks happy."

"Buttercup, stop that," Hannah said to the cat as she picked him up off the plant stand. She had to do a little pulling to get him to give up the leaf he'd been eating.

Buttercup is big and fat and orange with runny red

eyes. He's missing a part of one ear and the tip of his tail. Sometimes he smells just awful.

I'm glad I don't have pets.

"You didn't obey my orders, Brandon," Hannah said.

"You didn't give me any," I objected.

"I told you to be quiet. I—"

Suddenly Hannah stopped talking. Her eyes got really big, and she sort of smiled. Those are all signs that she's getting an idea.

Not all her ideas are what you would call good.

"Now we can play prison!" she exclaimed.

"Yes!" I agreed. "Yes! I want to be the guard!"

"You have to be the prisoner because you're the one who didn't obey orders," Hannah explained.

"What? Buttercup should be the prisoner," I said. "He's the one who did something wrong. And gross."

Mrs. D. came to the family room door. "You guys are going to have to play something that doesn't make so much noise," she told us.

Hannah smiled at me. "Prison is a very quiet game."

"Good," I said. "Then we should be able to watch TV while we play it."

MYSTERY GUESTS

Chapter 2

One Wednesday afternoon when we got off the bus at Hannah's house, her mother wasn't waiting for us next to the street the way she usually does. Instead, she was standing by the front door.

"Come on in, guys!" she called. "We have company!"

"Who could it be?" Hannah asked.

"We'll find out when we get into the house," I pointed out.

"Maybe it's a movie star who wants to use our house in a movie," she said. "Or maybe it's someone from a secret government agency who wants us to help with a special mission."

"Ah . . . I don't think so," I replied.

"A private detective?" Hannah suggested. "A lawyer who's here to tell us someone very old we've never heard of died and left us a million dollars in his will? Oh! I know! A king has sent a messenger to let us know that we're related to his family! I may be a princess!"

I told her not to get her hopes up.

Hannah went on and on trying to guess who we would find in the house. She didn't even come close.

A woman was sitting at the kitchen counter when we got inside. She had short hair that was a strange shade of red. Her lipstick was another kind of red. The big shirt she was wearing with blue jeans was *another* red. Silver hoops dangled from her ears. A tiny gray dog was standing on her lap. And *he* was wearing a red collar. His eyes looked big in his little head. He kept running his pointed little nose over the kitchen counter as if he was looking for something.

I decided it would be a long time before I ate anything at that counter again.

"This is my daughter, Hannah, and our friend Brandon Russell," Mrs. D. said to the woman. Then she said to us, "Hannah and Brandon, this is Mrs. Cooper. Her family has moved into that house behind ours."

"Do you have any kids?" I asked her. "Especially boys?"

"Is your house haunted?" Hannah asked at almost the same time.

Mrs. Cooper just stared at Hannah. Her little dog did, too.

I wanted her to answer my question before Hannah started in about haunted houses. A haunted house is the kind of thing she can talk about for a while. So I rushed to say, "You got any boys at your house?"

"Oh, we love boys at our house," Mrs. Cooper said, which wasn't what I'd asked her. "Don't we, Bucky?" she said to her little dog, who answered her with a great big yawn. "I have two wonderful boys. One of them plays two musical instruments, and the other one speaks three languages. They're both Eagle Scouts. They've never given us a moment of trouble. They're away at college now," she added sadly.

I was sad, too. I was hoping for a younger kid, maybe someone in third or fourth grade at the most. Someone who didn't spend all his time playing musical instruments or talking in languages I didn't understand. Someone who might not have a lot to do on Monday, Wednesday, or Friday afternoons. Someone who might come hang out in Hannah's yard. With me.

Things like that happen on TV all the time.

"Have you seen any ghosts yet?" Hannah asked Mrs. Cooper.

Things like that happen on TV all the time, too.

"Of course not," Mrs. Cooper replied. She frowned down at Hannah.

Hannah didn't notice.

"Has your dog seen any ghosts?" she asked. She looked at the dog as if he might answer her.

"Bucky doesn't see ghosts," Mrs. Cooper said.

"How would you know?" Hannah asked. Her eyes got big, and she started to smile. "Bucky talks, doesn't he?"

"No!"

Mrs. D. laughed. "Anything is possible to Hannah. Talking dogs. Tap-dancing horses. Singing cars. Magic bathtubs."

I remembered the magic bathtub. The water turned you into different people. You got out of the tub, and you were a cowboy or a ballerina or something.

It also poured chocolate milk from its hot water faucet.

Mrs. Cooper said, "Hmmm. My boys were never interested in things like that"—in a way that I could tell meant that if her boys weren't interested, no one should be. Hannah just kept right on talking, though.

"That house you live in has been empty for years and years," she said. "Since before I was born. Why wouldn't anybody buy it? Because it's haunted!"

"No one would buy the house because there was water in the cellar," Mrs. Cooper told her. "We got a very good deal on the place." She picked up her dog and kissed him on the side of his bony little head. "Didn't we, Bucky Boy?"

Bucky Boy didn't act like he cared about their good deal.

"Maybe someone drowned in your cellar and her ghost is down there," Hannah suggested. "Once when Brandon and I were outside playing ghost hunters, we heard a woman screaming in your house. I bet it was a woman who drowned, and now she keeps screaming for help."

I didn't want Mrs. Cooper giving me the old evil eye the way she was giving it to Hannah, so I said, "That was Mrs. Sunderland we heard screaming. She lives next door to you. She was yelling at her kids."

Mrs. D. told us to go wash our hands and then come back for a snack.

A CARTOON RAT WITH A COLLAR

Chapter 3

"Isn't this great?" Hannah whispered to me while we were both standing around the bathroom sink, trying to get the soap away from each other. "Someone has moved into that haunted house. And now we know her!"

"What would be great would be if someone with kids our age moved into that house. Someone with *boys*. And maybe a really good TV."

"She's got a dog, though," Hannah said. "Maybe she'll let us play with him. We can have adventures with him."

I don't know what kind of adventures she thought we could have with Mrs. Cooper's dog. Bucky looked like a cartoon rat with a collar. He sure wasn't going to drag anybody out of a burning building. He didn't even look as if he could run for help without stopping to take a couple of naps along the way.

I think Bucky's size must have been on Hannah's mind, too. When we got back to the kitchen, she went up to Mrs. Cooper and said, "How big will your dog get when he's grown up?"

"Oh, my Bucky *is* grown up. This is as big as he's going to be," Mrs. Cooper answered.

I thought she seemed to like talking about Bucky, so I asked, "You sure he's a dog?"

That was just the kind of question you should never ask around Hannah.

"Maybe he's a dog but a space alien took over his brain," she said. "I read a story where that happened. That wouldn't explain why he doesn't grow much, though. Or," she continued, getting another idea, "maybe *he* is an alien.

Maybe alien dogs are small because there's not much room in spaceships."

I got a little carried away then and added, "Maybe alien dogs have scary black eyes that pop out of their heads like your dog's do because they shoot laser beams out of them."

"Bucky is a purebred Chihuahua," Mrs. Cooper explained. "His father was a champion."

"What do you have to do to be a champion Chihuahua?" Hannah asked. "Could Bucky's father do tricks? Can Bucky do tricks, too?"

"He doesn't look like he can do much," I said.

"Brandon! Hannah!" Mrs. D. said as if we'd

done something bad instead of trying to chat nicely with a visitor. "You know it's rude to talk about how people look."

"But we were talking about her dog," Hannah pointed out.

"Or to talk about how their pets look. How would you like it if someone said Buttercup had scary black eyes that looked as if he could shoot laser beams out of them?" Mrs. D. asked.

"That would be so cool," I said. Buttercup would be a lot more fun if he could do that.

"Is Buttercup your dog?" Mrs. Cooper asked. She sounded worried, as if another dog might do something awful to Bucky. Like eat him.

"Buttercup is just a cat," I explained.

"He's not *just* a cat. He's our enemy. But don't worry. I can always defeat him," Hannah said.

"Bucky is afraid of cats," Mrs. Cooper said as she gave her little dog a hug. "He gets very upset when cats are around."

"Buttercup is only dangerous to houseplants," Mrs. D. told her. Then she waved her hand toward the front of the house. "Besides, he's sleeping in the family room now."

Bucky turned his head where Mrs. D. had pointed and pulled his lips back from his tiny pointed teeth. He looked as if he knew what was in the family room, and it didn't scare him a bit.

"Speaking of the family room," Mrs. D. continued, "Hannah and Brandon, it's time for you to take your crackers and oranges in there while Mrs. Cooper and I finish talking."

"Can we take the dog with us?" Hannah asked.

"Why?" I wanted to know.

"He can play cave explorer with us. He can save us from cave creatures," Hannah explained.

"Only if the cave creatures are really little," I said.

"I don't think Bucky would like doing that sort of thing," Mrs. Cooper warned us. "He's very delicate, you know."

Bucky started chewing on the edge of the kitchen counter with his pointy, delicate teeth. He growled at Mrs. Cooper when she tried to stop him.

"I think it would be better if Bucky stayed with us," Mrs. D. suggested.

Mrs. Cooper leaned over and whispered to me, "He really doesn't care for girls. He likes boys, though. That means he likes you."

A cartoon rat liked me. Yuck.

"I know!" Hannah said, turning to me. "*You* can be the dog!"

I had to think about that for a minute. Then I asked, "Will the dog get to save somebody?"

"Me," Hannah said.

"So the dog saves *you*, and *I'll* be the dog, so *I'll* get to save you."

I wanted to make sure I had that right, because I hardly ever get a part that good in Hannah's games.

"Yes," she agreed.

"Okay! Let's go!"

"Wait. We have to find Buttercup first," Hannah said.

"Why? You just said I was going to be the dog."

"We need something for you to save me from. Butter-cup will be a mountain lion that chases me into a cave. Then you can fight him off so that I can escape."

Fighting with Buttercup. My part in the game wasn't that good after all.

TURKEY
HUNTERS

Chapter 4

"Uh-oh," I groaned when I walked into Hannah's family room one day after school. "You've been to the library again."

Hannah goes to the library all the time. But does she ever bring a video home for us to watch? No. Only books for her to read. And then the first thing you know, she's got some new game for us to play.

When Hannah's been to the library, it usually means trouble for me.

"Wait till you see what I found," she said. She picked up a book from a big stack next to the sofa. She turned a couple of pages and then held up the open book in front of me.

"There are way too many words in that book," I told her. "And the words are all too long."

"Don't look at the words," she said. "Look at the picture."

The picture was much better.

"Dinosaurs!" I shouted.

"And what do the dinosaurs look like?" she asked.

"Dinosaurs!" I repeated.

"You said that. What else do they look like?"

I told her she was going to have to give me a hint.

"*Look* at them," she said. "There are a bunch of grown-ups in a line with some little ones mixed in. Where have we seen that?"

"At school when we line up to come inside after recess?" I guessed. "Except there are more kids than grown-ups at school."

"Nobody at school looks like a dinosaur! I'm talking about here in our yard," Hannah said.

"Oh. Oh! Turkeys!"

Hannah rolled her eyes and said, "Finally."

A few rows of trees separate the houses on Hannah's street. Behind the houses there are more trees before you get to more houses. Somewhere in all those trees a flock of turkeys lives. We only see them when the birds walk across Hannah's lawn or cross the street to get to someone else's yard. Sooner or later, they always disappear into the trees again.

No one knows where they come from or where they go.

And the turkeys do line up just like the dinosaurs in Hannah's library book.

"We're going to be dinosaur hunters just like those people who find dinosaur bodies buried in rocks," Hannah announced. "Except we'll hunt for turkeys."

"You mean we're going to look for dead turkeys? Cool!" I replied. "Except your mother won't let us leave your yard. What are the chances of us finding a dead turkey so close to your house?"

"Why would we look for *dead* turkeys?" Hannah asked. "Why would we want to find a big dead bird?"

"Because dinosaur hunters find dinosaur *bodies*—dead dinosaurs. You just said so," I reminded her.

"But that's only because there are no live dinosaurs now for them to find. We've got live turkeys, so we're going to look for them."

"What are we going to do when we find them?" I asked.

Since the dinosaur hunters only found dead dinosaurs, Hannah wasn't going to find any library books that would explain what to do with a live one.

"That's the great part. I've got it all figured out. The turkeys are going to be a herd of plant-eating dinosaurs like the ones in this picture," she said, holding up the book again. "We're going to save them from a meat-eating dinosaur."

I didn't think that sounded too bad. "Can I be the meat-eating dinosaur?"

Hannah just shook her head and started calling, "Buttercup! Buttercup, come here, kitty, kitty, kitty!"

I could tell what she was planning, and I didn't like it. "You're going to let Buttercup be the meat-eater, aren't you? Why can't I do it? I know I can be a better meat-eater than he can."

"Have you ever killed something and eaten it? Guts and all?" Hannah asked.

I had to admit I hadn't.

"Buttercup has. He's perfect for this part," she said. She started checking the room for all the spots Buttercup liked to curl up and sleep. "Buttercup!" she called again.

Mrs. D. came to the door to the family room. "He went outside. When the weather's good, he likes to go outdoors instead of using his litter box."

"Your meat-eating dinosaur is out pooping in the woods, Hannah. Maybe I should replace him," I suggested.

"No. No, this will work even better. The meat-eating dinosaur is already on the trail of the plant-eating dinosaurs. We'll have to find the *plant*-eating dinosaurs first so we can save them from the *meat*-eater. Or we'll have to find the *meat*-eater before he finds the *plant*-eaters. Either way, now we have more dinosaurs to hunt for."

"Oh, if only I had my dinosaur gun," I said, looking at Mrs. D. and trying to look sad.

"She's never going to let you bring your guns here, so just forget about it, Brandon. Come on," Hannah ordered. "We've got to get outside. There's no time to lose."

"Don't leave the yard," Mrs. D. reminded us as we ran out the door.

I headed right for the edge of the woods and started looking at the ground.

"Find any tracks?" Hannah asked, coming up beside me.

"Nope." I leaned down and picked up a long stick that curled a bit at one end. "But another dinosaur hunter dropped his weapon." I slid my hand along the side of the stick and made a *ka-kung* noise. "And it's loaded."

"Good work. Let's start hunting over by the driveway," Hannah said. "Then we'll look all the way around the yard."

When Hannah hunts for something, she likes to start at one end of the place where she's searching and hunt all the way to the other end. She does everything in order. But that takes forever, and it's boring. Besides, we were hunting for turkeys. They may not be as large as real dinosaurs, but it still doesn't take a lot of looking to see them.

By the time Hannah got to her driveway, I was already in the woods that bordered her yard. I went all around her property before she got to the side of her house.

"They aren't here today," I told her. "Game's over. I wonder what's on TV."

"They're not here because you scared them away shouting, 'See anything?' 'See anything yet?' 'Any sign of them?'" Hannah complained.

"Well, they're still not here. Let's go watch TV."

"They're here somewhere," Hannah said. "I'm sure of it."

Hannah thinks that if she's sure something will

happen, it will. Like turkeys will suddenly appear just because she wants them to. Like turkeys can tell what she's thinking. Or care about it.

"Look around, Hannah. Do you see any turkeys?" I pointed up. "Look in the trees. It's too early for them to be sleeping, so they aren't up there, either."

Because Hannah never does anything I say, she didn't look up. She looked down. Then she looked over at me and smiled.

"They've gone to their underground city," she said.

"What?"

"All those times no one knows where they are, they're underground," Hannah explained. "They've got tunnels and a palace down there."

"A turkey palace?"

"And turkey tunnels. And a turkey hospital and a turkey school and turkey stores," she continued.

Well, that was news. But it didn't change anything. "If they're in their underground turkey city, they're still not here. We should go see what's on—"

"No! We have to look for the door to their city," Hannah said. "They have a turkey firehouse and a turkey police department and a turkey water park and—"

"We're supposed to find a door to this underground city?" I broke in. "A real door with a doorknob? Here in the trees? That would be *creepy.*"

I do like creepy things.

I started running around kicking at the old leaves on the ground and trying to move rocks. If there was a door to an underground turkey land in Hannah's yard, I wanted to be the one to discover it. Then not only would I be a turkey hunter, I'd also be an explorer. It would be like playing two games at once.

"You're never going to find anything that way," Hannah said. "We need to get up high so we can see the ground from above. We'll be able to see a lot more that way. We need . . ."

"What?" I asked when Hannah stopped talking so she could think harder. "What do we need?"

THE MEAT-EATING DINOSAUR

Chapter 5

"We need . . . a helicopter," she declared.

I love helicopters.

We both turned and ran toward a big tree in the little strip of woods that separated the Dufranes' yard from the yard of the house in back of them. The tree had a fat trunk, low branches, and little boards nailed onto its side that we could use for steps. Once when we were playing "Jack and the Beanstalk," Hannah got her father to nail the boards there. She was sure Jack must have done the same thing himself when he was climbing his beanstalk or he would never have made it to the top.

"Here," I said, giving Hannah my dinosaur gun. "Hand this up to me after I'm on board."

The lowest branch of the tree was big and stuck out a long way, so it was perfect for two people to sit on. Once I was up there, I started making *woo-woo-woo-woo* noises like the ones you hear helicopter blades making on television. Then I leaned down so Hannah could pass my weapon up to me and climb up the tree, too.

We both sat there for a while and kept going *woo-woo-woo-woo*. But I got tired of it because our helicopter wasn't really going anywhere. And we still weren't seeing any doors to the underground turkey city. At least, I sure wasn't.

"I don't see anything," I said.

Hannah stopped making helicopter noises just long enough to say, "We've just started looking."

So I looked a little longer and said, "I still don't see anything."

"Wait! Do you hear what I hear?" Hannah asked.

"A dog yipping?"

" 'A dog yipping?' " she repeated. "How could you think that's a dog yipping? It's a giant dinosaur roaring!"

"It sounds like a dog to me," I said. "A really small dog."

"It sounds like the dinosaur is over by Mrs. Cooper's haunted house," Hannah went on. "Turn around and look."

We swung around so we could see into the yard right behind Hannah's.

"Wow! It's a meat-eating dinosaur," she whispered. "You see it? Over there? Behind that little wire fence by the deck?"

Not only did the meat-eating dinosaur sound a lot like a small dog, it looked a lot like a small dog. Or a big cartoon rat. Or Bucky. He was jumping up and down, wildly barking at the trees between his house and Hannah's. Lucky for us, someone had built him a pen.

"What's that thing behind the fence with him?" I asked. "It's a little house, isn't it? With windows and shutters and a little chimney? And look! There's a wire going from the Coopers' big house to Bucky's little one. That dog's house has electricity! He's got electric lights. Maybe that dog's got a little TV!"

"That's not a little house," Hannah said. "It's the doorway to the turkey's underground city. If that monster finds the plant-eating dinosaurs before we do, he'll eat them all."

"Hannah, most of the turkeys are bigger than that . . . thing . . . is," I pointed out. "Buttercup is bigger than that thing is."

"Think how much bigger that dinosaur will be after he's eaten a whole flock of turkeys," she said.

"That's true," I agreed. "But what can we do about it? We're not supposed to leave your yard."

"You'll have to shoot the dinosaur with your dinosaur gun," Hannah told me.

Okay! She didn't have to tell me twice. I lifted my stick up to my shoulder and took aim.

"Hurry up," she urged me. "If he goes through the gate, we'll never get him."

"He keeps jumping up and down," I complained. "He won't hold still."

"So push that special button on your gun that makes it hit things that are moving."

That was a good idea. But I was still having trouble pulling the trigger.

"I hate to shoot something that's so little," I admitted.

"You never mind shooting Buttercup," Hannah said.

"Buttercup isn't little. Not for a cat. Besides, Mrs. Cooper said Bucky likes boys. How can I shoot something that likes me?"

Hannah made a snorting noise that pretty much said what she thought about Bucky's feelings for me. Then her eyes got big, and she cried, "Wait! I know! Shooting that dinosaur isn't a problem because your dinosaur gun won't kill him. It doesn't shoot bullets. It shoots darts that are covered with a medicine that will turn meat-eating dinosaurs into plant-eating dinosaurs. Then they won't be dangerous anymore."

"Not bad," I said as I raised my gun again.

I went *Pow! Pow!* just as Mrs. Cooper came out of the house, calling to Bucky.

"What's wrong, Bucky Boy? Is there something out in the woods? Is there something bad out in the woods?" Mrs. Cooper asked her dog.

"It's just us," Hannah called. "Hannah and Brandon."

Mrs. Cooper picked Bucky up out of his pen and walked toward the trees at the back of her yard. You could see her looking around, trying to find us.

"What are you doing up there?" she asked once she saw that we were in a tree.

"Brandon's shooting your dog," Hannah explained.

"Not really! All I've got is a stick."

Mrs. Cooper was not the kind of person who would like to have someone shooting her dog.

"Your dog is a dinosaur," Hannah started to explain. "A meat-eater. One of those big, scary, ugly ones with blood dripping down all over it. You see, the turkeys that live in the woods look just like little dinosaurs . . ."

Mrs. Cooper sort of crossed her arms over Bucky and started nodding her head while Hannah talked, as if she wasn't really listening but just waiting for her to finish. She looked kind of mad. Hannah doesn't see mad looks very often. Most grown-ups smile at her and tell her how clever she is because she reads so many books and thinks up so many games. Hannah didn't know what a mad look was or that you really should shut up when a grown-up gives you one.

". . . so we're looking for them the way dinosaur hunters look for dinosaurs. Only *our* dinosaurs have a city under the ground. The door to their city is that little house in your yard. And—"

"That is not a door to an underground city. It is Bucky's house," Mrs. Cooper said. "And you better stay away from it."

Hannah didn't know you should shut up when a grown-up talks to you with the kind of voice Mrs. Cooper was using, either.

"Bucky is a meat-eating dinosaur. If he goes into the city, he'll eat all the other dinosaurs. So we have to turn him into a kind of dinosaur that doesn't eat meat. Brandon's gun does that."

"Do you think I'm a fool?" Mrs. Cooper asked.

I didn't think she really wanted us to answer that question. But Hannah must have thought Mrs. Cooper wouldn't have asked if she didn't want one of us to say something. So she said, "We think you're Mrs. Cooper."

"I know what you're doing here, young lady," Mrs. Cooper said. She made her eyes into little slits and leaned toward Hannah. "Bucky is not a dinosaur. He is a dog. The turkeys don't look like dinosaurs. They look like turkeys. And you are sitting out here teasing my dog and making him bark."

"Why would we want to do that?" Hannah asked.

"We didn't even know Bucky was in your yard until we heard him barking," I added.

Hannah's eyes got big. "Maybe he was teasing *us!*"

Mrs. Cooper gasped and said, "My boys would never dream of speaking to a grown-up like that when they were your age!" Then she took a big breath and said, "If you don't leave my dog alone, you'll be in very big trouble. I'm going to take Bucky inside where he'll be safe."

"He was safe in the yard," Hannah shouted after Mrs. Cooper as she walked away with her dog in her arms. "Unless the turkeys got him."

Mrs. Cooper had shifted Bucky in her arms so that his little rat face hung over her shoulder like a baby's. He looked as if he was laughing at us.

We forgot that we were supposed to be up in a helicopter looking for the door to an underground turkey city and climbed down from the tree. When we got to the ground, we could hear something moving nearby.

"*Now* the turkeys come back," Hannah said.

But when we looked for them, we didn't see turkeys at all. We saw Buttercup coming out from the trees. His tail was up, and his hair was all fluffed out. He was staring into the Coopers' backyard.

"Looks like Buttercup doesn't like Bucky." I laughed.

"I bet Buttercup was here all the time," Hannah

said. "That dog wasn't barking at us at all. He was barking at Buttercup."

I could tell Hannah felt really bad about what Mrs. Cooper said to her. For a while, anyway. But then she turned to me with a smile and those big eyes of hers and said, "There are two meat-eating dinosaurs living next door to each other now. You know what that means, don't you?"

"No."

"It means that someday there's going to be a dinosaur war."

I hoped I'd be there when it happened.

TRAPPED

Chapter 6

"There's a wolf at the door!" Hannah shouted one afternoon.

On TV wolves only live in forests where there aren't many people. Hannah's house isn't in a forest, and lots of people live near her. So I didn't think it was very likely there was a real wolf outside the glass sliding door in her family room. I didn't even look up from the fort I was trying to make with her mermaid and princess LEGO sets.

Then I heard the growling.

"What's that?" I asked.

"You never listen to me," Hannah complained. "I told you, it's a wolf. He's starving because it's been snowing for weeks, and he can't find anything to eat. He's trying to break into a human's house because he's desperate."

"Hannah, it's May," I said as I got up and went over to where she was standing, looking out through the door. "It hasn't been snowing for weeks. Not even for days. Not even for minutes."

"Pretend we're living in a part of the world where there's snow all the time," she explained.

"Like the North Pole? Hey, maybe the wolf is trying to break into Santa's Workshop!" I suggested. "Rudolph could use his antlers to chase him away."

Then I saw Bucky standing out on the deck. He was growling and hopping around on his short, skinny legs.

"What's he trying to do?" I asked.

"He's trying to claw his way into the house so he can eat us. Help me move some chairs against the door so he can't get in," Hannah ordered.

I wasn't too worried about Bucky eating us or

even getting into the house. But I love to move furniture, so I grabbed a chair and started to push it across the room.

I may have made a little too much noise, because Mrs. D. came in from the kitchen and said, "What's going on in here?"

"Wolves, Mom. Wolves! There's one on the deck trying to break in so he can eat us. And there may be more up on the roof trying to get down the chimney."

Hannah stopped talking and looked up at the ceiling. Mrs. D. and I knew there wasn't anything up there. But Hannah always acts so sure of the things she's saying. You just find yourself following along with what she's doing because *maybe* there's a wolf on the roof. And *maybe* it will come down the chimney.

So we both looked up at the ceiling for a few seconds, too.

There wasn't much to see, so then Mrs. D. asked us how Bucky ended up on her deck. "Little dogs usually stay indoors all the time."

"He must have escaped from his pen in the Coopers' backyard," I said. "He has a little house in that pen, you know. A little house with electricity. I think he may even have a TV."

"Oh, I heard about that," Mrs. D. replied. "They've got a lightbulb in there because he's supposed to be afraid of the dark."

Hannah smiled and her eyes got big. "I know what happened. The ghost at Mrs. Cooper's place got into Bucky's little doghouse. And Bucky's lightbulb burned out."

"I saw that once on TV," I broke in. "When the ghost showed up, all the lights in the house went *pop* and everybody was left in the dark."

"And Bucky's afraid of the dark," Hannah went on. "And afraid of ghosts, too, of course. So that's why he's on our deck acting scared."

We all looked at Bucky. He was staring back at us, and he had his lips pulled away from his teeth in a big snarl. Or as big a snarl as a little dog can manage.

"That's how Bucky acts when he's scared?" I asked.

"No, I was right the first time. He's a wolf," Hannah said.

She started to move the coffee table up against the door.

"Leave the furniture where it is," said Mrs. D. "I'll take Bucky home."

She started to open the sliding door, but when Bucky saw it move, he lunged toward it and growled some more. Mrs. D. slammed the door shut.

"Maybe I'll call Mrs. Cooper and have her come get him," she suggested.

While she was in the kitchen using the phone, Hannah said, "Wolves are afraid of fire. We can keep him away with torches."

"We're not supposed to use matches, Hannah. How are we supposed to make a torch?" I asked.

"Out of yellow and red colored paper, of course," she said. "What's wrong with you? We can't have real torches in the house. We'd burn the place down."

I don't think wolves are afraid of pretend torches

made out of yellow and red paper. But since Bucky wasn't really a wolf, it didn't matter. And I do like scissors.

When Mrs. D. came back to the family room, Hannah had all her paper spread on top of the coffee table.

"I can't call Mrs. Cooper," Mrs. D. said. "Her telephone number is unlisted, so the operator couldn't give it to me."

Bucky yipped and jumped up and down as Mrs. D. walked past the door.

"We'll just have to ignore him," she told us. "The dog will go home when he gets tired. Or hungry."

"He's already hungry, Mom," Hannah said as she taped some yellow and red strips of paper together. "That's why he's here. To eat *us.*"

She got up and ran over to the door so she could wave her paper torch at Bucky.

I don't think she was scaring him. But she might have been making him mad.

Hannah threw her torch on a chair and said, "You

know what we should do? We should start a fire in the fireplace and put a big pot of water in there to boil. Then if he comes down the chimney like in *The Three Little Pigs,* he won't be able to jump out of the fireplace and get us."

"Sweetheart, don't worry. Bucky is not going to come down the chimney," Mrs. D. promised.

"Oh, I'm not worried," Hannah said, smiling.

Mrs. D. laughed and told us she was going to go do some work on the computer.

"Can we go outside and play?" I asked. "Maybe Bucky just wants us to go out and play with him."

"Brandon," Hannah said, "no one goes outside and plays with a wolf. That's just stupid."

I flopped down on the sofa. "So the dog's keeping us prisoner in here?"

"Oh, good idea!" Hannah said. "Maybe we should plan an escape. You could go out and fight with the wolf while I climb out through the roof, jump down onto a snowbank, and run to a neighbor's cabin miles away to get help."

"How long would that take?" I asked.

"Maybe a half a day," she replied. "If I don't get lost in the blizzard."

I thought about that for a while. How long would a pretend half day last? Because if Hannah was busy for a long time in another part of the house with her escape plan, I might be able to watch some TV while she was gone.

I didn't get a chance to try because Buttercup came into the family room from wherever he'd been hanging out. He stopped dead in his tracks when he saw Bucky looking in through the glass sliding door. His back and tail went up in the air and his hair fluffed up. Out on the deck Bucky started shaking. I wondered if maybe he thought Buttercup was the ghost from over at Mrs. Cooper's house. But it turned out he wasn't shaking because he was scared. He was just getting ready to start barking louder than ever.

Bucky barked while Buttercup crept closer and closer to the glass door. Buttercup batted at the glass once and figured out that the little dog couldn't get through it. He stayed all fluffed up, but he didn't try to attack Bucky or fight him off. Instead, he marched back and forth in front of the door to make sure Bucky could see that he was there, just out of his reach.

Buttercup really is a monster cat.

"What's wrong with that dog now?" Mrs. D. asked as she ran into the family room. "Oh, dear," she said when she saw Buttercup.

"A wildcat broke into the cabin, Mom," Hannah said. "Now we've *got* to escape."

I was really getting tired of the wolf game. I said I would carry Buttercup upstairs so he couldn't bother Bucky.

"No, you won't," Mrs. D. said. "You don't want to go near a cat when he's ready for battle like Buttercup is right now. He'll think you're an enemy and fight you. And you probably won't win."

"But then we could play hospital," Hannah said hopefully.

Hospital is not one of my favorite games.

"Okay. This is what we're going to do," Mrs. D. told

us. "The car is in the driveway. We're going to go out the front door, get into the car while Bucky is back here, drive over to Mrs. Cooper's, and tell her to come get her dog."

"Oh, wow," Hannah said. "We really *are* going to escape."

While Bucky kept on barking his head off, Mrs. D. got her keys. The three of us went out the front door together. We had gone around the corner of the house and were almost to the car when Hannah yelled, "We're not going to make it!"

"What do you mean?" Mrs. D. asked, stopping to look at her.

"Wolf!" Hannah shouted, pointing.

Bucky had come around the house and was tearing down the driveway straight toward us.

THE
BIG BAD WOLF

Chapter 7

"Run!" Hannah screamed.

Hannah practices screaming a lot, and she sounds very realistic when she does it. If she screams "Run," everybody runs.

We got through the front door and slammed it shut just in time for Bucky to hit it with a little plop.

"I hope he's okay," Mrs. D. gasped.

We could hear him barking away on the other side of the door, which meant he was.

Buttercup slowly walked down the hallway to the front door. He stared at the door as if he could see through it and hissed.

"This is crazy," Mrs. D. said. "The two of them are

going to carry on like this for the rest of the afternoon. Maybe I can get out the back door now and run over to Mrs. Cooper's while Bucky is in the front yard."

"No, Mom, no," Hannah cried dramatically, throwing herself on her knees and wrapping her arms around her mother's legs. "Don't leave us."

We both stared at her with our mouths open. When nobody said anything for a while, Hannah looked up at us and said, "I read that in a book."

"I thought so," Mrs. D. replied.

"Me, too," I said.

Mrs. D. was just heading toward the back of the house when we heard a truck pull into the driveway.

Hannah and I ran to the window.

"It's the UPS truck," I announced. "You must be getting a package."

By the time the UPS driver was getting out of the truck, Hannah had a window open.

"Wolf! Wolf!" she shouted to the man. "Run for your life!"

I guess she thought that would sound a lot better

than "Tiny dog! Tiny dog! Run for your life!" But the UPS guy still acted as if he couldn't understand what she was talking about.

Until he saw Bucky running down the driveway toward him. Then he said a dirty word, turned around, and ran back to his truck. Just a minute later he was pulling out of the driveway and taking off up the street.

With Bucky right behind him.

"We're saved!" Hannah said.

We were playing wolf hunter out in the backyard when we saw Mrs. Cooper get out of her car. She was carrying Bucky in her arms.

We ran to the very edge of Hannah's family's property to see what was going on.

"Where did you find him?" Hannah called.

Mrs. Cooper came stamping across her lawn toward us.

"How did *you* know he was missing?" she asked. She had that mad look on her face again, the one she always seems to have when she sees Hannah.

"He came up on our deck and was barking and barking," Hannah explained. "He tried to get into our house to eat us. Then Buttercup got all upset. And *then* the UPS truck came. Bucky tried to kill the driver. You should have seen how scared that guy was. But he got away, and Bucky chased his truck down the street."

"Hannah, I am not in the mood for one of your foolish stories right now," Mrs. Cooper said.

That made it sound as if sometimes she *was* in the mood for Hannah's stories. Not whenever I was around.

"Someone stole Bucky!" Mrs. Cooper exclaimed.

I said, "Why would anyone want him?" and then felt bad about it, because Mrs. Cooper looked as if she was going to cry. If she did, I was planning to head back to the house in a hurry.

I felt even worse when I saw that Bucky was lying in her arms with his eyes closed.

"Is he . . . is he . . . dead?" I asked.

I hadn't ever seen a dead dog before. It was hard not to stare.

"No, he's just napping. I found him sound asleep

on a stranger's lawn. On your street," she added, looking at Hannah.

"He probably wore himself out chasing the UPS truck," Hannah explained. "For such a little dog, he can really move."

"How could he possibly have chased a UPS truck out of *your* yard when he was in his pen in *my* yard?" Mrs. Cooper snapped.

"He must have jumped out," I said. "You need a bigger fence."

"We'll help you build one," Hannah offered.

"He did not jump over the fence. He's much too tiny and weak to do anything like that. He was stolen," Mrs. Cooper insisted. "He must have escaped and been confused and lost. That's why he ended up at your house. He was trying to find his way home. Poor, poor Bucky," she sobbed just before she walked away.

If Bucky really was stolen, I don't think he escaped at all. I think whoever took him let him go. I know I sure would have. And I would have promised never to steal again.

PIRATE LIFE

Chapter 8

"What did you bring for our treasure chest?" Hannah asked me one day after we took off our backpacks at her house.

"Nothing."

Hannah sighed. "I knew you'd forget."

I didn't forget. I just didn't bring anything.

"It's a good thing I brought enough treasure for both of us," Hannah said.

I knew she would.

She led me over to her toy box. On top of it were the cardboard swords and knives she said we had to make when I was at her house a couple of days before.

She also had some red and blue bandanas, an eye patch from the Halloween costume she wore the year before, a couple of belts, a long cardboard tube like they use in rolls of gift wrap, and a big piece of black construction paper with a white skull painted on it.

"That's not the pirate flag I made. What happened to mine?" I asked. "The one with the bones under the skull?"

"It looked awful, so I threw it away and made another."

"What! I copied the picture right out of your pirate book," I reminded Hannah. "What do you mean it was awful?"

"Brandon, you just can't draw. Everyone knows that."

"No one complains about my drawing except for you," I said.

"All those other people are just being nice," she replied.

She should try that sometime.

Hannah moved everything off the top of the toy box so she could open it. Then she reached in and pulled out a big, square, purple and silver cookie tin.

"Look at this!" she said eagerly when she took the lid off.

On top of a pile of that shredded silver foil people put in gift bags was a necklace made from a long string of shells. Next to that were some old rings and some fake pearls Hannah uses when we're playing that she's a rich person and I'm her butler.

"That's pretty crummy treasure," I said.

"Then next time you'd better bring something yourself," Hannah replied.

I guessed her stuff didn't look that bad.

She closed the box and tucked it under her arm. Then she handed me the swords and bandanas and picked up the paper flag.

"Can't I carry the treasure chest?" I asked.

"I'm the captain," Hannah explained. "I get to carry the treasure chest."

"Then I'll be another pirate who tries to steal your treasure from you," I said.

"No, Buttercup's going to do that," Hannah explained.

"Then who am I going to be?" I wanted to know. "One of the guys who mops the deck?"

"Yes," Hannah said on her way to the kitchen, where her mother helped us put on our bandanas.

Mrs. D. tied the bandanas so that the knots were behind our heads and not under our chins. No pirate wears a bandana tied under his chin. She also said I would get to wear the eye patch first because I was company.

Hannah hardly ever pays attention to the company-first rule.

"And if that horrible little dog comes over here, you come right inside," Mrs. D. said when she was finished working on us.

Hannah's eyes got wide and she started to smile. "Since Bucky lives in a ghost house, if he comes over here, he can be a ghost ship that we have to escape from."

"And you escape from him into our house, Hannah," Mrs. D. repeated. "He's little, but he has plenty of nasty little teeth. And he's got nasty little toenails. He could hurt you."

"If he keeps coming over here, are we going to have to stay inside and watch TV?" I asked hopefully.

"If he keeps coming over here, I'll have a talk with Mrs. Cooper," Mrs. D. promised.

"If Bucky *does* come over here again, you should tell Mrs. Cooper you're going to call the police, Mom," Hannah suggested. "They could come and arrest Bucky."

"They'd have to catch him first," I said.

We found Buttercup stretched out on a sunny spot he'd found on the family room floor. He refused to get up by himself, so while Hannah carried all our pirate stuff, I got stuck lugging him outside. He got to play the part I wanted in Hannah's pirate game, *and* I had to give him a ride outside so he could do it.

"You know what we need?" Hannah said after I let Buttercup go near the edge of the lawn so that maybe he'd wander off among the trees. "Pirate names."

"Yes!" I agreed. "That would be so cool."

"And we need a shovel so we can bury our treasure," she added. "You'll find one in the garage."

"I guess I have to dig the hole, too, huh?" I said when I got back from my errand.

"I'm the captain," Hannah reminded me. "Captains never bury treasure themselves. They tell someone else to do it. Besides, you love digging holes."

That's true.

I jammed the point of the shovel into the ground, but Hannah stopped me before I could start work.

"You can't bury the treasure here." She pointed to the tree we were standing next to. It was the big tree with the board steps nailed on the side. "You'd be burying it right under our ship."

"But that's a good idea," I said. "It would be easy to get to it that way."

"But, Brandon, there's nothing but ocean under

the ship. You can't bury treasure in the ocean. Bury it under those bushes near the edge of the woods. That's an island," Hannah insisted.

Digging the hole took longer than it should have, because Hannah kept telling me I was doing it wrong. When I finally finished, we were able to strap on our belts over our clothes and stick our cardboard swords and knives into them. Then we climbed up the tree.

"I thought of a pirate name for you while you were digging," Hannah said when we were both sitting on the lowest limb.

"I don't even get to think of my own pirate name?" I complained.

"Your name will be Deadeye, because you wear an eye patch."

"Yes! Yes! If my name is Deadeye, I should have to wear the eye patch all the time, shouldn't I?" I asked. That was how it sounded to me, at least.

"Yes, you should."

"Yes! Yes!" Then I started getting worried. "What's your name going to be?"

"Captain Hannah Trueheart."

"What kind of pirate name is that?"

"It's a *good* pirate name because I'm a *good* pirate," Hannah explained.

"And I bet you're going to have to be captain all the time because your name's *Captain* Hannah Trueheart," I said.

Hannah admitted that was true.

I tried to get the pirate flag to hang on a twig over our heads. When I'd finished with that, I said, "You know, there's not a whole lot to do to make this ship sail, seeing that it doesn't really go anywhere. And isn't really a ship."

"Hold on. I'm looking at something through my spyglass," Hannah said.

She was holding one end of the cardboard tube she'd brought from the house up to her eye so she could look through it.

"What are you looking for?" I asked.

"Bad Bart the Evil Pirate," Hannah answered.

"Oh. Buttercup."

"He's always in this part of the ocean at this time of day. He's a threat to all good pirates," Hannah said.

"Gee, Hannah—"

"Captain Hannah Trueheart," Hannah reminded me.

"Captain, is there any such thing as a 'good' pirate? Aren't we supposed to be bad?" I asked. "Stealing things? Burning ships? Making people walk the plank? Good people don't do things like that."

"But I don't want to be a bad pirate. I want to be a good one. And I am the captain," Hannah reminded me while she continued to look through her spyglass. "Uh-oh. Trouble."

"Bad Billy?" I asked.

Hannah corrected me. "Bad *Bart*. No, it's not him. It's a ghost ship."

I turned and looked toward Mrs. Cooper's house. I didn't need a spyglass to see that Bucky was in his little pen.

"Has he been there all the time we've been outside?"

Hannah nodded her head. "I thought he was just a rock in the pen, but then he moved and now he's standing up."

"Does he see us?" I asked.

"I don't think so."

"If he starts barking at us, Mrs. Cooper will get mad and say we're teasing him. Maybe we should go back inside now," I suggested.

"Shh. We need to escape before the ghost ship sees us," Hannah whispered.

I didn't think a ghost ship could *see* anything. I didn't argue with her, though. I just started to climb down from the tree. I was already bored with playing pirate and escaping sounded like a good idea to me.

Hannah grabbed me. "I didn't mean escape that way," she said, while still whispering. "I meant we need to sail our ship away."

"Our ship is a tree limb, Hannah. It's not going anywhere."

"Be quiet, Deadeye," Hannah ordered in a low voice.

"You're going to give us away. Do you know what will happen if the ghost ship catches us?"

"No."

"It will be just awful," Hannah explained. "Put up the sail."

"How do I do that? We don't really have a sail here."

"Come on, Brandon!" Hannah shouted. "Do I have to tell you everything!"

Captain Hannah Trueheart must have given our location away to the ghost ship, because it started barking at us.

"Oh, no," I said. "Mrs. Cooper's going to be out here any minute. Turn around, Hannah. Don't look at him. Maybe she won't blame us if she sees we're busy looking at something in your yard."

Except Hannah wasn't busy looking at something in her yard. She was busy staring into the Coopers'.

"What's he doing?" she asked.

I turned around and looked. Bucky was running

back and forth in his pen from the side that was farthest away from us to the side that was nearest.

Hannah answered her own question. "He's going to run right into the fence if he's not careful."

"No, he's not," I told her. "He's going to jump it."

And he did. Sort of. He flew up into the air and hooked the top of the fence with his front legs and hung there for a second. Then he used his tiny back legs to climb up the little squares of wire until he was at the top.

"He's going to get all tangled up in the fence if he tries to jump. If he gets stuck, should we go over and help him?" Hannah wondered. "We're not supposed to leave the yard, but—"

"Oh, my gosh! Look!" I cried. "He got over the top! He's out of his pen!"

"And he's coming right for us! Run for the house!" Hannah screamed.

The Cat Always Gets the Best Parts

Chapter 9

I didn't even bother using the little steps to get down from the tree the way I usually did. I just swung over the side of the limb and dropped to the ground. Hannah, though, had to make a great big deal out of it. She stood up on the limb and jumped. That meant she had a longer ways to go before she hit the ground. When she did, her legs crumpled up under her and she fell down.

In the meantime, Bucky was still running right for us. His little tiny legs were a blur, they were moving so fast. All he'd be able to get hold of on me was my feet. But Hannah was lying on the ground. He could get hold of lots of her.

"Get up!" I shouted.

"I can't," she moaned. "I think I broke my back. Or my leg. Or my elbow. No, it's my bottom. I think I broke something in my bottom. It hurts."

Any minute, Bucky was going to be right on top of her with his nasty little teeth and his nasty little toenails.

"I'm coming, Captain!" I shouted.

My plan was to throw myself on top of Hannah so that Bucky would have to chew on me before he could get to her. I was going to save her. It was going to be great.

But just as I landed on her, an orange, furry ball shot through the air and crashed into Bucky.

We heard a lot of spitting, growling, yipping, some howls, and then the sound of small feet hitting the ground as Bucky took off with a big cat right behind him.

"Buttercup!" I yelled. "You ruined everything!"

"Get off me!" Hannah roared, sounding as if her bottom felt much better. "You've got to go to the garage and get my wagon. We need it for my ambulance."

When I got back with the wagon, Hannah gave me a long list of commands for getting her into it. When I didn't move her fast enough to please her, she just got up and jumped into the wagon herself.

That was when Mrs. Cooper started running around her yard, calling, "Here, Bucky, Bucky, Bucky. Come on, baby! Come back to Mama!"

"We're getting out of here," I told Hannah. I started pulling her and the wagon back toward her house.

Hannah's a lot heavier than she looks. The wagon was so loaded up with her that it kept getting stuck on roots and sinking into dips in the lawn.

"You're driving the ambulance all wrong," Hannah kept saying.

"If you're so sure you know how to do it, why don't *you* get out and pull the *ambulance?*" I asked. "I'd be a much better accident victim than you are."

Suddenly, we heard Mrs. Cooper shout, "Hold it right there." She wasn't using the kind of voice she uses when she's talking to Bucky, so we figured she meant us.

"Was that your cat that chased Bucky out of my yard?" Mrs. Cooper snapped at Hannah.

I guess she didn't notice the ambulance.

Hannah groaned and tried to lie down at the bottom of the wagon.

"Yes, yes," Hannah whimpered weakly. "Buttercup saved me."

"Saved you from what?" Mrs. Cooper demanded.

"A . . . a . . . mad . . . dog," Hannah said. Then she groaned again, let her head drop to one side, and closed her eyes.

"She means Bucky," I told Mrs. Cooper once it was clear Hannah didn't have anything more to say.

Mrs. Cooper got kind of mad herself. "Bucky isn't *mad*. He's had all his rabies shots. Besides, he was in his pen . . . until someone let him out."

"She means us, Hannah," I said. "I can tell by the way she's looking at us. Her eyes are almost closed, and her lips have almost disappeared because she's pressing them together so hard."

Hannah sat up just long enough to say, "He got out by himself." Then she dropped back down in the wagon and closed her eyes again.

"I don't think he likes it in that pen. Maybe that's why he's so mean whenever he gets out and comes over here," I suggested.

"Bucky? Mean?" Mrs. Cooper sputtered. "That just can't be. My Bucky is a little sweetheart."

"Mrs. Dufrane said that if Bucky came over here we were supposed to come right inside. She was afraid he'd bite us," I said.

"Oooo," Hannah groaned. "She may call the police. Oooo."

"The police!" Mrs. Cooper repeated.

She finally looked down at Hannah.

"What's wrong with you? Are you okay?"

"Don't worry," Hannah moaned. "Buttercup saved me from Bucky. I don't know what I would have done if Buttercup hadn't been there to chase him away."

"What do you mean?" I asked. "I would have saved you."

Hannah opened her eyes and looked at me. "No, you wouldn't have."

Mrs. Cooper started to say something but was interrupted by someone calling her from her backyard. A man was waving at her from beside a car.

"I think that's the minister at the church we just joined," Mrs. Cooper muttered. "I wonder what he wants."

I think he wanted to talk to her because he started walking across Mrs. Cooper's backyard toward us. He smiled and waved again as he got closer. Suddenly, he came to a stop, staring at something over to his left. Then he shouted a dirty word, turned around, and ran back to his car.

Bucky was right behind him.

Mrs. Cooper took off, all the while yelling, "Bucky! What are you doing? Do you want to play? He just wants to play, Reverend Tedford! *Bucky!*"

We watched her while she struggled to pull Bucky away from the minister, who was trying to climb up onto the hood of his car. He didn't look as if he wanted to play. Not with Bucky. Not with anybody.

I tried to prop the handle of Hannah's wagon against her leg so I could go around to the back and push. That was even worse than pulling because no one was steering.

"Well, Buttercup's back," I said as I walked around to the front so I could start pulling again. "I guess he's too big and fat to run for very long."

"Oh, bring me my little pet," Hannah said.

"Get him yourself," I replied.

"I'm hurt, Brandon! Bring me my cat!"

Running after little dogs must be hot, sweaty work, because Buttercup stopped halfway across the lawn to take a bath. At least I didn't have to chase him. I picked him up, carried him over to where Hannah was lying in the wagon, and dropped him on her stomach. She grunted and then wrapped her arms around him.

"You were so brave, Buttercup," Hannah said as if she was talking to a baby. "You were such a hero."

"He's not a hero, he's a cat. Cats fight with dogs," I told her. "He just did what cats do."

But Hannah didn't seem to hear me. Her eyes were getting big.

"Now we can play television reporter! I can be a reporter talking to the cat hero!"

"Who will I be?" I asked as I went back to pulling the wagon.

"You'll be the guy who runs the camera and takes pictures of the hero," Hannah said.

"What?" I looked over my shoulder at Buttercup and said, "The next time a dog attacks somebody, *you're* going to take pictures of *me.*"

Hannah started to smile. "The next time a dog attacks someone, he'll be a robot dog. No weapons will stop him. The only way to defeat him will be to spray him with a garden hose so he rusts!"

I love garden hoses.

"Can I be the dog?" I asked.

GAIL GAUTHIER has written six books for middle-grade and older children. She began working on a story for younger kids after her husband gave their niece (who shares her home with a number of cats) an amazing Venus flytrap for her birthday. While trying to write picture and chapter books about a girl, a cat, and a plant, Gail slowly created the character Hannah. But it wasn't until Brandon burst onto the scene that *A Girl, a Boy, and a Monster Cat* finally took its present shape. Only one sentence from all the previous drafts made it into the book, and the amazing Venus flytrap wasn't in it.

Gail's niece, who was four when she inspired this book, will be eight when it is published. Learn more about Gail at www.gailgauthier.com.